The Cap That Mother Made

Prentice-Hall, Inc.,
Englewood Cliffs, New Jersey

The Cap That Mother Made

adapted and illustrated by
Christine Westerberg

Printed in the United States of America • J

Prentice-Hall International, Inc., London
Prentice-Hall of Australia, Pty. Ltd., North Sydney
Prentice-Hall of Canada, Ltd., Toronto
Prentice-Hall of India Private Ltd., New Delhi
Prentice-Hall of Japan, Inc., Tokyo
Prentice-Hall of Southeast Asia Pte. Ltd., Singapore

10 9 8 7 6 5 4 3 2

Library of Congress Cataloging in Publication Data

Westerberg, Christine, 1950—
The cap that mother made.

SUMMARY: When Anders wears the cap his mother made, he receives quite a bit of unusual attention.
[1. Fairy tales. 2. Folklore—Sweden.
3. Hats—Fiction] I. Title.
PZ8.W515Cap 813′.5′4 [398.2] [E] 76–48301
ISBN 0-13-113365-9
ISBN 0-13-113274-1 (pbk.)

This is the story of Anders, and his ad – ventures in and out of the deep, dusky Swedish forest. It begins one day long,long ago, when Anders got a new hat. What a hat it was: soft, fuzzy wool,with reindeer marching all around the edge. Anders' mother had made it just for him.

Anders went out for a walk in his new hat. Soon he came upon a giant ash tree, and under it a man resting in the shade. But when the man saw Anders he jumped up, smiled, and bowed until his whiskers brushed his knees.

"Hmmmm . . ." thought Anders, "I must look even handsomer than I thought. Perhaps good enough to see the King!" He turned to ask where the King lived.

But the man had vanished.

Anders wandered on, and by and by he met a little girl who could not resist going up to touch the beautiful reindeer.

"I'll trade my hat for yours. And I'll give you the kite, too," she said, tugging on a great yellow kite.

But not for a hundred kites would Anders give up the cap that Mother made.

"Give you my hat?
My beautiful hat?
No, I cannot.
I cannot do that."

And he waved good-bye and went on his way.

A little later he met a unicorn. It looked at his hat, then rolled its eyes and tossed its mane and said, "Bless my tail, what a terrific hat! I'd give my own horn for such a hat."

But Anders shook his head.

"Give you my hat?
My beautiful hat?
No, I cannot.
I cannot do that!"

"Just for five minutes?"

Anders shook his head.

"I will give you a ride to the Silver Castle."

"And then will you promise to give my hat back?" Anders asked.

"Of course," said the unicorn.

"Hmmm . . . the Silver Castle . . ." murmured Anders.

"You see," the unicorn whispered, "I live in the palace yard."

"Ahhh, the Silver Castle . . ." Anders sighed again. "How beautiful. I was just going there myself." So he

climbed on the unicorn's back and they were off, flying through the trees like the North Wind.

But as they swooped over a puddle, they heard a small green frog croak, "What a wonderful hat! I'd give my biggest wart for such a hat."

But still Anders was firm.

"Give up my hat?
My beautiful hat?
No, I cannot.
I cannot do that!
Besides, your head is too small. It would never fit you."

But Frog's face drooped, and his beady black eyes filled with tears. Anders felt terrible.

"Well, I guess you could wear it, in a way," he said. "But only for five minutes."

And so the three friends sped off to the Castle.

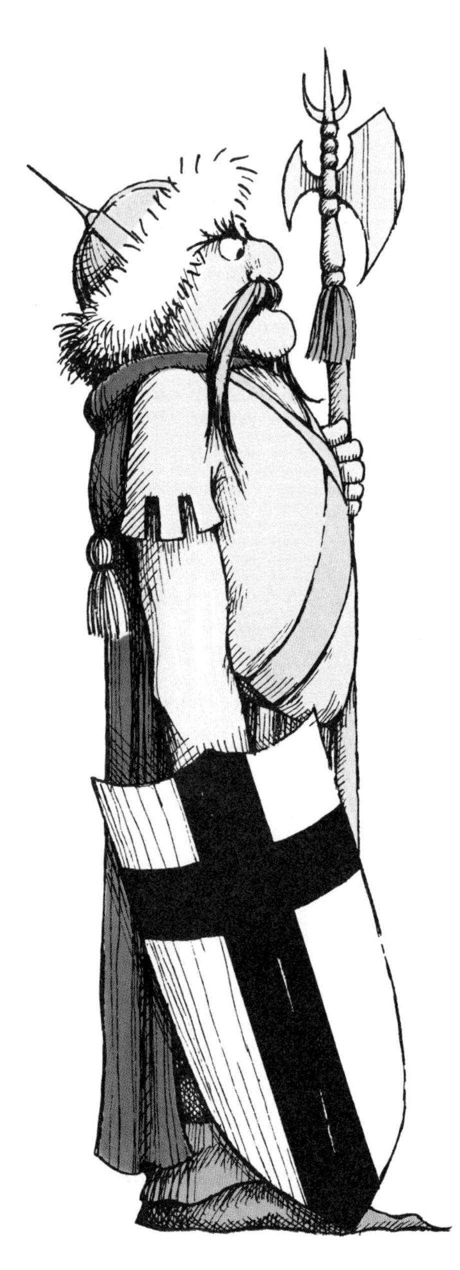

But at the gates, the guards would not let Anders in.

"Princes only," they snapped. And that was that. Poor Anders could see the splendid people bustling about inside; he could smell the delicious smells of the royal dinner, but he could go no further.

He turned to leave, but as he walked sadly away from the Castle he heard a voice call, "Let him in! Let him in! His hat is princely enough!" The startled guards jumped and almost dropped their swords, and out danced the princess, elegant in satin ribbons. She stepped down gracefully, then grabbed Anders by the hand and whisked him into the banquet hall, where his mouth dropped open in amazement. What sights! What smells!

"What a hat!" she cried. "What will you take for it: cookies, candy, cakes shaped like cats and kittens, lollipops like lions, brownies like . . ."

"No, no, Your Highness, stop!" Anders interrupted.
"Leave me my hat,
my beautiful hat!
I won't take it off.
I cannot do that!"
He grabbed it and pulled it down over his ears.

The commotion roused good King Olaf, who loved hats himself—he had one hundred and twenty-nine crowns—to reprimand his daughter. "Hush," he said. "Anders does not want your crown."

"But perhaps," he added, "he would like mine."
Now fear filled Anders' heart and weakened his knees.
The gleaming crown was coming closer and closer, and he knew that he could *not* say no to a King.

Then he remembered something. He bowed deeply, swept the cap off his head . . .

And by the time King Olaf was able to sit up again, the three friends were far, far away, flying through dusky forests and over high mountains like the South Wind.

Then it was time to say good-bye for the day, and at home, Anders' brothers could hardly believe their ears.

"You fool!" they groaned. "With the King's crown you could have bought a hundred hats, and soft leather boots besides, and a horse . . . you could have bought anything in the world!"

"That is true," Anders replied, "but there is nothing in the world half as good as the cap Mother made me."

Anders' mother couldn't say a word. She just gave him the biggest, most loving bearhug.

Then she took out her wool and they started on a new hat for King Olaf, so that next time Anders went visiting he would have something to take along.